wild wind

Margaret Scariano

A **HIGH ADVENTURE** BOOK
High Noon Books
Novato, California

Cover Design and Illustrations: Herb Heidinger

International Standard Book Number: 0-87879-409-3

9 8 7 6 5 4 3 2 1 0
3 2 1 0 9 8 7 6 5 4

High Noon Books
a division of ATP
20 Commercial Blvd.
Novato, California

Contents

Chapter 1

First Things First

Katie Bradley stood at the kitchen sink. She hated it when Molly lost her temper. It never solved the problem. And we've had enough problems this year, Katie thought. It's true Molly is only in first grade. But she has to learn like everybody else. She can't stay home from school whenever she feels like it. I wish Dad would say something. Since Mother died last year, he's left it up to me to keep Molly in line. And I'm tired of it.

It isn't fair, Katie thought. I'm only her big sister. Why didn't Dad speak up? Tell Molly her 24-hour flu bug was gone. She was better and she had to go to school. But, no, he just shrugged his shoulders and left the breakfast table without eating. His face was red as if he had a fever. He moved slowly. Then Katie heard him call the school office. He told them he had the flu and would not be in to work. "You'll have to get someone to drive the school bus for me today," he said.

I hope it won't be me, Katie thought. I've got a ton of work to do on my desk in the school office. Katie had a license to drive the school bus. After she had finished high school, Dad had insisted that she get a license. "Gives you another skill, Katie," he had said.

The driving course had been fun. And she had done well. The next summer they asked her to drive the school bus during summer school.

Now Molly was stamping her foot. Katie felt like shaking her. She turned from the window and faced her. "Young lady, stop that! I don't care if you're a walking flu bug. You're going to school. And that's final. Now finish your breakfast."

Molly gave the table a shove. Her glass of milk tipped over. It dripped onto her dress and splashed on the floor.

"Now see what you've done!" Katie scolded. "What a mess! Why can't you behave?" She grabbed a paper towel and wiped up the floor.

Molly began to cry. "My dress is all wet."

"You can wear it anyway. I just washed that dress. You're so careless, so sloppy," Katie shouted.

Molly began to cry. "My dress is all wet."

"You don't like me." Molly jumped up from the table and ran to the bathroom.

What a way to start a morning, Katie thought. I should go tell her it's OK and give her a hug. She looked at the breakfast dishes still to be done. And she had to make the beds. Take the roast from the freezer for dinner. No time now.

Tonight she'd make up with Molly.

Quickly she gathered up the dishes. She washed them and stacked them in the rack to dry. She could still hear Molly sniffling. Maybe she should go to her. She walked down the hall toward Molly's room. She passed her bedroom. Darn! She hadn't made her own bed yet. She hated to come home to a messy room. She went into her room and made the bed. Then she started for Molly's room again. The telephone rang.

"Get the phone, will you, Katie?" Dad called from his bedroom.

As soon as she heard the principal's voice, she knew she would be driving the school bus. Mr. Peters said, "We need you to drive the bus this morning, Katie. All right?"

"Oh, no, Mr. Peters. Not today. Have you called anyone else?"

"I've called everyone I could think of, Katie," Mr. Peters said. "No one could come. It's this 24-hour flu bug."

"But I have reports to type for the school board. They want them tomorrow. I'll never get them done. It'll take an hour to drive the kids to school and an hour to take them home again." Katie stopped to take a breath.

"Katie, first things first. In my school the kids come first—then your work in the office. I'm talking about priorities—important things first."

Katie sighed. "Right, Mr. Peters. I'll be right over to get the bus."

She hung up the phone. "Molly, are you ready to leave for school? I'll give you a ride."

There was no answer.

Katie looked in Dad's room. "Did Molly leave?"

"Yep. Said nobody liked her. Everybody yelled at her. I asked her who *nobody* and *everybody* were. She said 'Katie.'" Dad peered over his glasses. "Ease up a little, Katie. Molly needs to feel she's loved."

Katie clenched her mouth tight. She didn't want any angry words to pop out. Finally, she said, "Molly needs discipline, Dad. Just like any other kid her age."

Dad nodded. "I know. I know. But you can catch more flies with honey than vinegar, Katie. Maybe if she knew you really cared about her, she'd try harder to behave."

"Right, Dad. Gotta go. I'm the bus driver for the east side kids today. See you at lunch." She leaned over and kissed his hot forehead. "Hope you feel better."

She drove her pick-up truck down the bumpy country roads toward the school bus yard. At least the roads are dry, she thought. The weather during the past month had been awful. Rain. Snow. Hail. Wind. Today it was warm and cloudy with no sign of rain. The air was still and heavy. She hated to drive in bad weather. And the kids. They seemed to be more restless and noisy in a thunder storm or blizzard.

She turned on the radio. The newscaster was telling about earthquakes in southern California. Hurricanes off the coast of Florida. Flash floods in New Mexico. "Mother Nature is not fooling around," the announcer said. "She's showing her power over man. That's the news. Stay tuned for some easy listening music."

Katie listened to the music. Dry roads. No mention of hurricanes, earthquakes or floods for their area. Maybe the kids wouldn't be too noisy on the bus today.

Chapter 2

Rumblings of Danger

Katie backed the school bus out of the yard. She glanced at her watch. She was on time. None of the kids would be late for school. And she'd be at her desk in the school office in an hour. With a little luck and no coffee breaks maybe she could finish the reports for the school board.

She drove toward the east side of town to begin picking up the children. At every stop she was asked the same question—"Where's Mr. Bradley?" And each time she explained that her father had the 24-hour flu. Some children groaned. Some of them said, "Tell him hello." Others said, "Too bad! He's a great guy. Tells funny jokes."

"I'll tell him. Now take your seats. We've got to get going," Katie said.

The children moved toward the back of the bus. Katie heard one of them say, "She's a real crank. Glad Mr. Bradley's only got the 24-hour flu. That means he'll be back soon."

Katie's hands gripped the steering wheel tighter. It was easy for Dad to be Mr. Nice Guy. He didn't have to worry about taking care of the house and holding down a job at the same time — or even disciplining Molly.

Someone yelled in the back of the bus. She heard what sounded like a fight.

She looked in the rear view mirror. "Hey, back there," she yelled. "Knock it off. Or get out and walk."

Silence. Katie could almost feel the kids' anger. She didn't care. Her job was to get them to school — not to tell jokes. The rest of the ride was quiet — an unhappy kind of quiet.

She let the children off in front of the school. Then she parked the bus in the parking lot in back of the school. As soon as she reached the school office, she began typing the reports for the school board.

At noon the principal, Mr. Peters, said, "Tell your Dad we miss him. Hope he's feeling better."

"I will, Mr. Peters." Katie looked up from her reports. "I'd like to work through the lunch hour. I might be able to finish the reports before driving the kids home after school."

"But what about your Dad? Won't he be expecting you for lunch?"

"Yes, but—"

"No buts, Katie. Those reports aren't as important as checking on your father. Now get going."

All the way home Katie mumbled to herself. Sure, she thought, Mr. Peters says the reports aren't important— but then he will suddenly want them. And Dad—he was all right. He really didn't need to be checked.

At home Dad was watching television. "How did it go, Katie?"

"Fine. The kids asked about you." She put her sweater on the back of the chair. "I'll fix you some lunch. You look a little better."

After his second cup of soup Dad said, "I've been watching television this morning. There's heavy rain forecast for this afternoon."

"I'll drive carefully, Dad."

"I know you will, Katie. But I was thinking. The little Larson boy is in the first grade. He gets out a half hour before the other kids. And he had the flu last week. Better have the bus in front of the school early. No need for him to get wet."

Great! That's all I need—to baby sit, Katie thought. But she smiled at her Dad. "Don't worry. I'll be there in plenty of time." She added, "If I can find Molly, she can ride the bus, and we'll come home together."

Katie knew Molly wouldn't want to ride the bus. She liked to walk home with her friends. She would never think about her clothes getting wet and dirty in the rain—or about who had to wash them. She and Dad just went happily along. Expecting their clothes to be clean. Expecting food to be bought and cooked. They never thought about *who* did all those things.

As Katie drove back to school after lunch, rain pelted her windshield. The sky was gray. The air was heavy. In the distance she heard rumblings of thunder.

She felt restless. Sort of jumpy. She knew she was a good driver. But still she didn't like slick, muddy roads. And the kids—if the weather were bad, they'd be monsters!

Chapter 3

Black Cloud Watch

All afternoon Katie typed as fast as she could. She wished the rain would let up. Then she wouldn't have to stop work to let Joey Larson onto the bus early.

The windows rattled. The wind blew the rain against the panes. A real spring storm. She looked at the clock. Almost 2:30. With a sigh she turned off her electric typewriter. She knocked on Mr. Peter's door. "I'm leaving now to drive the bus."

"Good, Katie. And thanks for helping out. Drive carefully. See you tomorrow."

Katie went out the back door. The wind blew rain in her face. She tucked her chin down and ran for her bus. It was all she could do to stay on her feet. The sudden gusts of wind whipped her skirt against her legs. It tangled her hair and threw her off balance. Finally, she reached the bus. She drove it around to the front of the school.

Joey Larson was waiting at the front door of the school. When he saw the bus, he ran to it. Katie opened the bus door.

Out of breath, Joey stood a moment in the doorway of the bus. Then he asked, "Are you Mr. Bradley's mother?"

Katie couldn't help smiling at the question. Sometimes she felt like she was mother to both Dad and Molly. But she answered, "No. Mr. Bradley is my father." She turned and looked out the side window.

Joey stood there a moment. Then he walked to the back of the bus.

Suddenly a crackling sound filled the bus. Katie jumped. She looked out the side window of the bus. Almost like slow motion a huge branch of an oak tree crashed to the ground. Katie heard Joey's small cry of fear.

But before she could say anything, the kids began pouring out of the school building. The rain was really coming down. Lightning flashed. Thunder shook the school bus. As the kids piled into the bus, they were quiet. As though the storm had scared them speechless.

Katie waited as long as she could for Molly to

come out. Finally, she asked, "Any of you kids see my sister, Molly? She's a first grader. Miss Blaire's class."

"I think I know her. Does she have long braids?" Joey asked.

"Yes. Did you see her leave the school?"

"She went out the back way. With, you know, her best friend."

There was nothing Katie could do about that. Surely, Molly would hurry right home. And it was only a few blocks.

Katie turned on the engine. She'd be glad to get these kids home. Already she was worrying about the roads. Just a little rain and the dirt roads turned to slick mud.

At the last stop light before leaving town, she waited for the green light. People, bent by the wind, hurried for shelter. Muddy water rushed along the curb. She shuddered just thinking about the five miles of bad road ahead of her.

The light turned green. She shifted gears and drove out of town. The wind seemed stronger in the country. Or was it because she felt alone on the lonely road? She smiled to herself. How could she be alone with a bus filled with kids?

The windshield wipers went back and forth. Still Katie leaned close to the windshield. It was hard to see with the rivers of water flooding the windshield. She glanced up at the sky. It was getting darker. She turned on the headlights. Even with the sound of the engine and the rain, she could hear the wail of the wind. She had to hold the steering wheel tightly. Often a gust of wind would hit the side of the bus. Then it was all Katie could do to keep the bus on the road. Now and then, the bus swayed from side to side.

At her first stop she pulled off the road onto a muddy strip. Three children got off the bus. "Run as fast as you can to your houses," Katie told them.

The wheels of the bus spun as she started to pull away. She let up on the gas pedal. Carefully she drove the bus back onto the main road. It wasn't much better. But at least there was no danger of getting stuck in the mud.

The storm grew worse. Lightning streaked across the sky. It lit up the bus. Thunder followed. One of the children yelled, "Wow. That was close." Others cried out in terror. Now Katie heard some of the younger children crying.

"Let's have it quiet back there," Katie said firmly. "I'll have you all home safely in a short while." She wished she felt as sure as her voice sounded. Now she was glad that Molly wasn't with her. At least she was home out of the storm.

Finally all the kids except for Joey Larson had been dropped off. Katie drove down the lane toward the Larson house.

"Miss Bradley," a trembling voice called out. "Miss Bradley."

"I can't talk with you now, Joey. I'm driving,"

A funnel cloud! Moving rapidly
in a whirling black mass toward them.

Katie answered.

"I won't talk. I just want to sit close to you."

Katie stopped the bus. "Sure, Joey. Come sit right behind me. I'll have you home in a minute."

A gust of wind hit the bus. It rocked back and forth. Joey gasped.

Katie gripped the wheel tighter. Boy! She'd be glad to park this bus. She stopped at a stop sign before turning into Joey's road. Carefully she checked the left. No cars. She looked to the right. No cars. Then she saw it.

A funnel cloud! Moving rapidly in a whirling, black mass toward them!

Chapter 4

Take Cover!

For a second Katie couldn't move. She saw the funnel cloud. She heard the roar of the wind. She felt the bus rock from side to side. Her mouth was dry and sour tasting. She could almost smell her own terror. She knew she had to act quickly. But still she sat. Frozen. Her eyes watched the dark cloud move toward them. The bus seemed to shiver from the noise of the tornado. Her foot pressed against the brake trying to stop the black cloud.

She shifted in the driver's seat as if to wake herself up from the nightmare. She had to do something. She couldn't just sit there—waiting. Her forehead was hot and sweaty. Icy fear made her breathing short and panting. She wanted to scream. Scream for help. But who would hear her? She was alone in this valley of disaster. Alone and waiting for the wild wind to blow her off the face of the earth. Then she heard a small voice.

"What's the matter, Miss Brady? Why aren't we moving? Are we out of gas?"

Joey! She had to do something. And now. She was responsible for his safety.

Fear and panic gripped her. Rules of what to do during a tornado raced through her head—take cover in a cellar—stay away from windows and outside walls. Then like printed words in her head she remembered. "If outside, take cover and lie flat in the nearest depression, such as a ditch, culvert, excavation, or ravine."

She knew she had to get out of the school bus. The tornado would destroy it. She turned off the engine. She opened the bus door. Then she turned around to Joey. "Give me your hand. We have to get out of here. Tornado!" She pulled him toward the open door.

Joey began to cry. "My homework! Miss Bradley. I've got to get my homework."

"Leave it. We have to get out of this bus."

But Joey jerked away and ran back to his seat. He grabbed a book with lined paper tucked between the pages.

Now a noise like the roar of a thousand hot-rods filled the air. "Come on, Joey. Hurry."

Katie reached out and yanked Joey off the bus. Half-dragging him, Katie ran for the ditch alongside the road.

She looked up at the funnel cloud again. It dipped toward the earth. It moved rapidly. Each second it got darker as the funnel picked up dust and rubbish along its outer ring.

Katie held Joey's hand tightly. She dove for the ditch—pulling him with her. "Lie flat, Joey. Keep your head down," Katie yelled. She put her arm across his back.

The air had a strange heavy feeling. A wet dirt smell filled Katie's nose. Her mouth was dry and tasted sour—like she'd been sick at her stomach. Underneath her arm she felt Joey shaking. Now a loud roar blocked out all other sounds. And a dusty smell filled the air.

Katie heard a whoosh. Carefully she peeked over the rim of the ditch. She saw the bus. It was rolling over and over. Then, as though a giant had picked it up, the bus was lifted off the ground and was tossed through the air.

Katie buried her head in her arms.

Chapter 5

No Sign of Life

It seemed as if she and Joey had been lying in the ditch forever. Like a nightmare she'd felt the pressure of the storm as it cut a path across the land. Her ears still rang with the sound of the wind. When the tornado passed over them, Katie thought her clothes would be ripped from her back. Now she was aware of silence. Deadly silence.

What do I do now, she wondered. I wish I could just lie here and pretend none of this had happened. Wouldn't it be great if it were just an awful dream? I wish I could go back to this morning and start all over again, she thought. No spilled milk. No hassle. No sick father. No storm. But that's not the way it is. I've got to pull myself together.

She opened her eyes. She raised her head carefully. The bus was gone. The land looked rumpled—like a messy room. She heard Joey whimper.

"It's over, Joey." Katie sat up. But Joey still lay flat in the ditch.

Gently Katie turned him over and pulled him into her arms. She patted his back and spoke soft words. "It's over. You're all right. I'm here with you."

"I know. I know." Joey said. "But my homework got all wet!"

"First things first, Joey." Katie smiled to herself. That's what Mr. Peters, the principal, had said to her this morning. This morning? It seemed like years ago. She gave Joey a hug. "You're safe, fellow. That comes first."

Joey still seemed unable to move. "Come on, Joey, I'll take you home. School to home delivery. That's what I offer."

Katie stood up and helped Joey to his feet. "Are you all right? No broken bones or cuts?"

Joey shook his head. Together they climbed out of the ditch.

"Where's the bus?" Joey's voice trembled.

"The tornado lifted it up and blew it away. We're lucky we got out."

Joey hugged his book with the wet homework papers close to him. "Yes, Miss Bradley. We sure

"It's over. You're all right. I'm here with you.

are lucky."

They started walking toward Joey's house. The land looked different. Old man Allan's water tank was knocked over. Power lines lay on the ground. Several wires touched and sparked. "Be careful not to step on any of those power lines, Joey." Katie kept a firm hand on Joey's hand.

Telephone poles lay on the ground. They looked like broken match sticks. Fences were down everywhere. Many trees had been uprooted. Those that were still standing had lost huge limbs. A steady rain was falling. The cloud was grey with thick clouds. But the lightning and thunder seemed over except for some rumbling in the distance.

"Where's the tornado now?" Joey asked.

"A long way from here. Tornados move fast." Katie wished Joey would move faster. She was anxious to get him home. Then she could get home, too. Make sure Dad and Molly were all right.

They passed the Smith's farm. It had lots of damage. Mr. Smith's silo was blown over. His barn must have been struck by lightning. It was almost burned to the ground. The house was gone. Just blown away. Just the steps were left. A cow was lying on the steps. Probably dead.

Farther on, they passed Martin's farm. One wall of the house stood. The pictures were still on the wall. Curtains hung from its one window. Katie thought it looked like a doll house. No roof and open at the front. A dog ran out from behind the one wall. It barked. It was still protecting the home even if only one wall was standing.

Just down the hill Katie saw Joey's house. At least, it was still there.

"You're almost home, Joey. See—there's your house."

"But where are my folks?" Joey began to shake again. "Did the tornado blow them away?"

Chapter 6

Missing!

A cold fear clutched Katie's heart. Where *were* the Larsons? The barn and chicken house were still standing. The house seemed OK. Had the tornado simply picked up the Larson family and dropped them in another county?

"Where is everybody?" Joey whispered. "Did they go away and leave me?"

"They wouldn't do that," Katie squeezed his hand. "Maybe they're all in the barn. Let's see. Besides your mother and father, don't you have a big brother, too?"

"Will. He's in high school." Suddenly Joey jerked on Katie's hand. "Come on. Let's hurry. I want to find my mother and father."

Half of Katie wanted to hurry. Wanted to turn Joey over to his parents. But the other half worried. Where were the Larsons? Did they get through the tornado unhurt? Katie shuddered.

What would they find?

Worried or not, she had to go on. Get Joey to his folks safely. And if the Larsons were hurt — or were not there? Well, she'd cross that bridge when she came to it. She was hoping they were safe, and she could borrow a car to get home.

Home. What would she find there? She tried not to think of the possibilities — the roof gone or Dad's truck blown over. She forced the thought of Dad or Molly being hurt from her mind.

They opened the gate to the barnyard. A tractor without its wheels sat near the gate. No dog ran out to greet them. The place looked deserted.

"Let's check out the barn first," Katie said. They poked their heads inside the dark barn. They called. No one answered.

They walked toward the house. The wheels to the tractor lay against the apple tree in the front yard. As they walked up the sidewalk to the front porch, the door flew open. Mrs. Larson stepped out.

"Joey!" She cried. She ran down the steps and hugged the little boy. "We were so worried about you. There's been a tornado."

"We were in it, Mom. It blew right over us, didn't it, Miss Bradley?" Joey smiled at Katie.

"Sure did. I'm Katie Bradley, the school bus driver." She told Mrs. Larson about the bus. How she and Joey lay in the ditch to get away from the tornado. "I'm so glad you are all right, Mrs. Larson. At first your place looked empty."

"We were in the storm cellar. Waiting for the wild wind to pass through," Mrs. Larson said. "Oh, my goodness! Where are my manners? Come in, Miss Bradley. I'll fix some coffee. You can dry off."

"No coffee, Mrs. Larson. But I'd like to call my father. I want to be sure he and my sister are all right." Katie followed Mrs. Larson and Joey into the kitchen.

Mr. Larson and Will sat at the kitchen table. Again Katie explained who she was and told them about the bus and the ditch. "Now I need to call home."

"There's the telephone. Hope the lines are still working," Mr. Larson said.

Katie's hopes faded. She remembered all the wires she and Joey had seen on the ground. But tornados were funny. Sometimes they destroyed everything on one side of a road. On the other side of the road nothing was damaged.

With fingers crossed for luck, she dialed the number. Moments later, Dad answered!

"Katie! Where are you?"

Katie told him where she was and about the bus. "But what about you? Everything all right at home?"

"Fine. Fine. We lost two trees, and the wind blew down the back fence. But that's all." Then he asked, "How about the kids? Did you get them all home safely?"

"Yes. Joey Larson was the last one on the bus. I walked him home."

Dad let out a sigh of relief. "Good girl, Katie. Good girl. Well, you and Molly hurry on home now."

"Molly?" Katie asked. Her heart began to pound.

"Yes. Isn't she with you?" Dad asked.

"No, Dad. I thought she walked home as usual." Katie tried to keep the panic out of her voice. She knew she sounded scared. She tried to remember what Joey had said. Something about Molly going out the back door of the school. Walking home with Ginny, her best friend.

"Get home as fast as you can. I'll call the police." Dad's voice sounded worried.

"Dad, wait. Don't get excited yet. Maybe Molly stopped at Ginny's house. Call there first." But Dad had already hung up.

"Something wrong?" Mr. Larson asked.

"Yes, my little sister didn't come home from school. We only live a few blocks away. She should be home by now." Katie tried to keep her voice calm.

"I'll give you a lift home," Mr. Larson said. "Will, bring the car around front."

"Sure, Dad." Will took off at a run out the back door.

"Thanks. I'd really be grateful for a ride," Katie said.

"We owe you that after all you did for Joey," Mrs. Larson said.

Katie started for the front door. "Wait, Miss Bradley. Wait." Joey ran to her and threw his arms around Katie's middle. "I was scared. But you made me feel better."

In the car Katie asked Mr. Larson to drop her off at the school. Her car was still parked there.

"That is, if the school is still standing," she said.

It was. But there was no one around. Her car was the only one in the parking lot. "Thanks for the ride, Mr. Larson."

"Sure you don't want me to wait? Make sure the car will start and everything?" Mr. Larson asked.

"I'm sure it'll be fine. No trees have fallen on it. Looks OK. Thanks and goodbye."

She unlocked the car and slid in. She was anxious to get out of the deserted lot. And very anxious to find Molly. Where was she?

Chapter 7

The Search

Mr. Larson waited until Katie had started the engine. Then he drove off. Katie sat a moment in the parking lot. It was good the tornado had missed the school. But where else had it touched down? Had Molly been sucked up in its center? Or was she lying hurt somewhere? Unable to get home?

Then another thought came to Katie. Maybe Molly was at Ginny's waiting for the storm to let up. She shifted the gears and started home. She'd better check with Dad before doing anything else. Maybe Molly would be waiting for her.

She drove down Third Street. Perhaps Molly had just gone off to play without reporting home first. Katie's hands tightened on the steering wheel. She'd better not have done that. Or — or she'd really get it. Katie swallowed hard. The lump of fear in her throat seemed to be growing.

Tears blurred her eyes. She knew it wouldn't matter what Molly had done—if she were just safe.

As she drove home, Katie saw lots of damage. A window had been blown out of the grocery store. Men were nailing boards to protect the store from the weather. A block from home she had to detour. A huge tree lay across the street. Some of its branches had caved in a garage roof. Telephone lines and electrical wires lay across the roof sizzling. There was a burning smell in the air. People were out in the rain trying to clear the street. Now she heard the fire engine's siren. Three houses from hers a van lay on its side—a victim of the wind.

Katie pulled into the driveway. At least, the house still stood. Her father must have heard her drive up. He came to the front door.

"Molly? Is she home?" Katie asked as she ran up the front steps. Dad didn't have to answer. His worried face gave Katie the answer.

"I called Ginny's house," Dad said. Katie followed him into the living room. "Molly wasn't there. She and Ginny walked home together. Ginny's mother tried to get her to come in and wait out the storm. But Molly said she had to get home. She was planning a surprise for her sister."

"Did you call the police?" Katie asked.

"Yes. They'll keep an eye out. But they're busy over at Webb's Rest Home. Lightning struck it. The police are helping to move the people to a motel. Guess there was quite a lot of damage." Dad sat down in the big chair. He covered his face with his hands.

"I'm going out and look for Molly. I'll start at the school. Follow the same route she would have taken." Katie buttoned up her raincoat again.

"I'll go with you." Dad stood up.

"No, Dad, you shouldn't get chilled."

Dad looked grim. "You think I'm worried about some darn chill?" His voice rose. "That's Molly out there." His voice cracked.

"I know, Dad. It's just that someone has to be here. You know, in case Molly comes home—or someone calls about her."

Dad sighed. His shoulders drooped. In a low voice he said, "Yes, of course. You're right, Katie. You go. I'll stay here."

At the front door Katie stopped. "Try not to worry, Dad. I'll check back with you in a little while." She closed the front door and hurried down the steps.

The worst of the storm had passed through. The winds had died down. A steady rain fell. Daylight was fading into dusk. Katie walked along the sidewalk toward the school. This was the route she and Molly usually took to school. But it seemed strange to Katie. As if something were missing. Then Katie knew what it was. It was the sound of voices—kids yelling, neighbors talking, friends visiting. Now there was a hushed sound—like in church or at a graveyard. Katie shivered. She pulled her coat collar up around her neck. A few people stood in their yards or driveways talking quietly.

Each time she passed anyone, Katie asked about Molly. But no one had seen her. As she passed the small city park, she heard a sound like a young child crying. Was it her imagination? She walked on. There it was again. She stopped and listened. The sound seemed to be coming from beneath some bushes.

"Molly." Katie spoke softly. "Is that you?" No answer. Katie started to walk on. She heard the cry again. She turned around and dived into the bushes. She reached toward the sound and grabbed. She pulled out a kitten. Its soft mew sounded like a young child's cry.

Just what I need, Katie thought. A kitten. It

seemed very young. Had the storm blown it away from its mother? She remembered that Molly had begged for a pet just this morning.

In fact, that had started the whole argument that ended in the spilled milk. And then my angry words, Katie thought. If she could just call back those words.

She remembered what Molly had said. "Even an ant farm would be fun to have."

And Katie remembered, too, what she had answered. "No pets. I don't want one more thing to clean up after." And she had pointed her finger at Molly.

Molly had said, "I'm not a *thing.*"

Katie scooped the kitten up. She unbuttoned her coat and tucked the kitten inside. Just its head peeked out.

Now she hurried on toward the bridge. A crowd of people were standing on the bridge. "What's wrong?" Katie asked a woman.

"Someone fell in. That's all I know."

Katie shoved her way through the people to the rail. She looked down into the creek. It was now a roaring river of muddy water. "Who fell in? Do you know? Who was it?" She asked a man standing beside her.

"Don't know. We heard that a couple of kids

She buttoned her coat and tucked the kitten inside.

were playing on the banks. One slipped and fell in." He shook his head. "No chance of survival. Nope. None at all."

"Who was it? A boy or a girl?" Katie asked.

The man looked at her. "Don't know. Be lucky if the searchers even find the body."

Another man spoke up. "I heard it was Sloan's

boy. I see Mr. Sloan and his wife talking to the rescue team over there now."

"How awful! Poor family." Katie left the crowd on the bridge with mixed feelings. Feelings of relief. It wasn't Molly. But feelings of sadness for the Sloan family.

At the school she walked around the building. Several times she called, "Molly?" But there was no answer. Where was she?

Chapter 8

Behind the Stuck Door

Now Katie was standing at the back door of the school. She tried to think the way Molly would think. What would Molly do in a bad storm? What kind of surprise had she planned for Katie? Where would she go if she were afraid? Katie fought to keep panic from jumbling her thoughts.

All right. I'll pretend I'm Molly on my way home, she thought. She followed the sidewalk around the building to the main street. She walked quickly. Now and then she called Molly's name.

She passed Ginny's house. When she came to the grocery store, she stopped. Would Molly go in there to get out of the storm? If she did, why wouldn't she have called home? Maybe she didn't have money for a phone call. Maybe she was looking around and lost track of time.

Katie walked into the grocery store to check. It looked strange with its window all boarded up. Inside it looked even stranger. When the tornado wind had blown out the window, it had also knocked over shelves. Cans of vegetables and fruit littered the floor. Broken bottles of syrup and oil were sticky to walk on.

Katie walked around the mess and went up and down all the aisles. No Molly. She asked the clerk at the check-out stand, "Have you seen a little girl with long braids?"

"Lady, you got to be kidding!" The clerk laughed. "I wouldn't have seen my own mother if she'd been here. That wind hit the window with a thud. And then the shelves fell over. Lots of noise and people rushing around!"

"Yes, I guess so." Katie turned to go.

"That's a cute little kitten peeking out of your coat. Yours?"

Katie hesitated a moment. Then she said, "My sister's." For some reason just saying that made her feel better. Like she was closer to finding Molly. She turned to go.

"Hey, lady, ask the store manager about your sister. He pays more attention to the kids than I do. Maybe she went in the laundromat next door."

Katie couldn't help laughing. "I hardly think so. She's never had any interest in washers and dryers."

"How about video games?" The clerk asked. "There are several games in the laundromat."

"Thanks. I'll check." Katie walked next door to the entrance of the laundromat. It wasn't likely that Molly had gone in there to play video games. In the first place, she didn't have extra money. And she had never seemed to want to play video games. Still, Katie would check every store in town if she had to.

Two policemen were working on the entrance of the laundromat. The door was jammed. They were trying to pry it open. Katie asked them if they had seen Molly.

"We think there's a child in the laundromat. A girl. We heard her calling for help," one of the policemen said. It shouldn't be much longer. We should have this door open in a minute. It got jammed when that telephone pole over there fell on it. It took a long time to move that pole." He stooped down again and began to pry the door.

Was it a waste of time to wait? Still, Katie didn't know where else to look. She stood to the side and waited. And waited.

It seemed to take forever. Finally the door

popped open. Katie looked in. There was Molly! Staring at her. For a moment she was stunned. Then she rushed to her sister and hugged her. "Oh, Molly! Molly!"

Molly was trying hard not to cry. Katie heard her sniffling. "I was locked in! And it was dark. The lights went out."

Katie looked in. There was Molly.

Katie saw how dark the large room was. Guess the storm knocked out the power in here, she thought. She turned to Molly. "You're all right now. Come on. Let's call Dad right away. He's been very worried." Katie took Molly's hand to lead her to the pay phone just outside the grocery store.

"I can't leave here." Molly pulled back. Tears were in her eyes. "I don't have my dress."

Katie stopped. "What do you mean you don't have your dress?" Katie was tired. She wanted to get home. Now what?

Then Molly really began to cry. "It was a surprise. I wanted to surprise you, Katie. Make you happy."

"Shhhh. It's all right, Molly." Katie led her to a far corner of the laundromat. "Now tell me. What was the surprise?"

"I can't tell you. Then it wouldn't be a surprise." Molly looked down at the floor.

"Well, I have a surprise for you, Molly," Katie said. "You tell me your surprise. And I'll *show* you my surprise. Is it a deal?"

"Honest? You really have a surprise for me?" Molly asked.

"Honest. Now tell me."

"Well, after I left Ginny, I decided to surprise

you and wash my own dress. You know, so you wouldn't have to do it. I had a quarter. So I came to the laundromat."

"And took your dress off in front of everyone?" Katie asked. That was hard to believe.

"No, Katie. Not in front of everyone. I went into the bathroom. Took off my dress. Then buttoned up my coat. I put the dress in the washing machine. I was waiting for it to dry in the dryer. But the lights went off. And my dress is still wet. And the door was stuck." She began to cry again. "And I was scared."

"It's all right now, Molly. Don't cry. Or — or you'll make your surprise sad." Katie unbuttoned her coat and pulled out the kitten. "Here." She put the kitten in Molly's hands.

"Mine? I can keep it always?" Molly's eyes were wide.

"You can keep it always. What are you going to call it?"

"That's easy. I'll call it 'Surprise.' That's a good name."

"It sure is. Now let's get *my* surprise out of the dryer. Then we'll call Dad and tell him that we're on our way. We can dry your dress at home."

"Let's call Dad first. I want to tell him about

Surprise."

At first Katie thought it would save time to get the dress and then call Dad. But then she thought about the storm. And the damage and sadness and worry it had caused. Then she knew. Some things just had to come first.